MIRROC
THE GOBLIN SHARK

With special thanks to Andrew Taylor

For Henry

ORCHARD BOOKS

First published in Great Britain in 2016 by The Watts Publishing Group

1 3 5 7 9 10 8 6 4 2

Text © 2016 Beast Quest Limited.
Cover and inside illustrations by Artful Doodlers with special thanks to Bob and Justin
© Orchard Books 2016

Series created by Beast Quest Limited, London

The moral rights of the author and illustrator have been asserted.

A CIP catalogue record for this book is available from the British Library.

ISBN 978 1 40834 068 4

Printed in Great Britain

Orchard Books
An imprint of Hachette Children's Group
Part of The Watts Publishing Group Limited
Carmelite House, 50 Victoria Embankment, London EC4Y 0DZ

An Hachette UK Company
www.hachette.co.uk
www.hachettechildrens.co.uk

MIRROC
THE GOBLIN SHARK

BY ADAM BLADE

ORCHARD

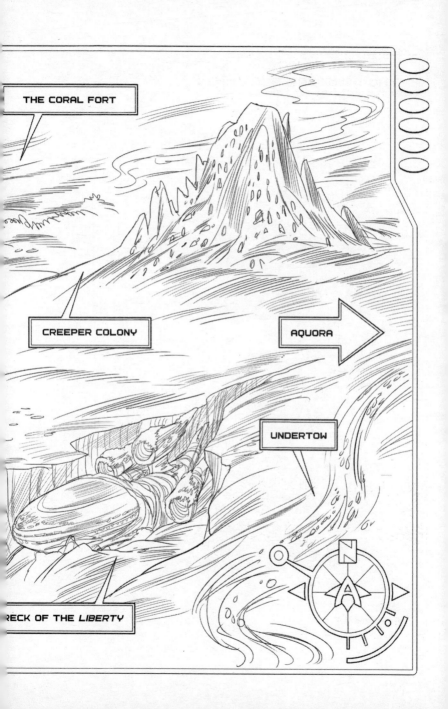

>TRANSMISSION FROM THE STARSHIP
LIBERTY

Any who threaten the SS *Liberty*
must die.

For 2,000 years I have lain at the
bottom of the ocean, forgotten.
For 2,000 years I have guarded my
ship. But my duty will never end:
analyse, react, destroy. Time may
have corroded my circuits, but I
have only grown more determined.

Now I have built four weapons to
aid me in my mission – creations
so powerful, nothing can stand
in their way. Enemies of the SS
Liberty beware. I will never stop
hunting you.

All threats must be terminated!

CHAPTER ONE

MYSTERY MOUNTAIN

Max sat back in the pilot seat of the sail sub and watched the mutated plant life of the Primeval Sea rushing by. He sighed happily – the current at their backs was quick and steady. The sub's flexible metal sails were formed into a cone, catching the water stream and driving them forward.

The Sepha were as good as their word, thought Max.

The Sepha were Merryn-like creatures of

the Primeval Sea, able to whip up strong currents like the one Max was riding now. But as the sub sped onwards, the Sepha were already dwindling in the rear-view monitor. Like so many friends made in the oceans of Nemos, they had to part too soon. Seconds later, they were completely gone from sight. Max noticed Rivet, his pet dogbot, was watching the Sepha disappear as well.

"It's okay, boy," he said, giving the dogbot a pat on his rounded head. "We'll see them again someday."

"Yes, Max!" said Rivet, his titanium tail wagging.

"Woo hoo!"

The excited cry came through loud and clear via Max's headset. He grinned to see his friend Lia in the shimmering current ahead. She was riding her swordfish, Spike, making him leap in the stream. As Spike executed

one more joyful leap, she raised her coral spear in a webbed fist.

"Enjoying yourself?" Max asked through his communicator.

Lia laughed. "This is a whole lot more fun than trying to ride the Undertow! I could do this all day!"

She made Spike loop again. Max thought

how good it was to have some time to relax at the end of another dangerous adventure…

But a red flash on his energy tracker reminded him that their current mission was far from over. They were approaching the third of the four scattered elements from the starship *Liberty's* engine. These elements were the only things that could restart the power core of his home city, Aquora – unique items brought to Nemos on the starships carrying the original planet colonists. The *Liberty* had crash-landed on Nemos centuries before, but it was the starship's insane artificial intelligence, Iris, that had scattered the elements across the Primeval Seas. They had been lost for centuries…until now.

The thought of the elements made Max check the drawer with the storage container. He was relieved to see Flaric and

Magnatese, the two elements he'd collected already, gleaming safely in their sealed compartments. Iris had been using these incredible sources of power to drive two of her all-powerful Robobeasts. *Until we shut them down,* thought Max, closing the drawer again carefully.

Iris was a dangerous enemy, although for reasons known only to itself, the computer had chosen the holographic form of a twelve-year-old girl. She was desperate to get the coordinates to Aquora from Max so she could destroy the city.

That is not going to happen, he thought, and turned his attention back to the tracker. The ping was coming faster and louder now, indicating a signal getting stronger.

"I hate to spoil the party," said Max, "but I'm picking up the Blinc's signal." He adjusted the sail sub's course in line with the tracker, his heart beating faster at the thought of the danger to his home. With the power core out of action, the water filters would stop working. The people of Aquora would start dying of dehydration – a slow, painful end for his family and friends.

"Another element!" Lia exclaimed, pushing Spike harder to keep pace with the vessel. Max didn't need to tell her the importance of their mission.

But at that very moment the pace of the sail sub started to slow.

"The current is dying!" said Lia.

A moment later it ceased completely. The sail sub's engines kicked in to compensate for the reduced drive coming from the sails.

"We're reaching the limits of the Sepha's Aqua Powers," said Max, watching the glowing plants and coral, mutated by radiation from the crashed starship, passing by more slowly. "We're on our own again from here."

Rivet gave a worried growl.

"Don't worry, boy," said Max and checked his tracker again. The red signal was starting to flash even faster, indicating that they were getting very close now. "Whatever's up ahead, we're ready for it…"

His voice trailed away as a gigantic shape loomed through the waters ahead. On first glance it looked like a huge, undersea mountain. But as the sub drew closer, Max saw that its sides were smooth and clear, as if they had been polished. It dwarfed everything in sight.

"It's like a giant crystal." Lia gasped. "How beautiful!"

The reflective sides of the mountain caught the glory of the sea in all directions, reflecting a million different shades and colours. The sail sub and Lia on her swordfish were reflected too – tiny specks amidst the vast ocean.

"Beautiful can be deadly," Max said. He examined his energy tracker and wasn't surprised to see that the object was lit up

as a huge source of power, with the centre glowing brightest. Something in there was throwing out a massive amount of energy. It could only be the Blinc – the third element.

"So we'll be careful," said Lia.

Max nodded and pushed the throttle on the sail sub, powering towards the crystal mountain. Drawing closer, dozens of circular openings in the reflective surface became visible.

"There could be anything in there," Lia said as she followed the sub towards one of the openings. Max could hear the nervousness in her voice, and that made him worried.

"We don't have a choice," he said bravely. "Stay alert."

The sail sub passed through the opening into semi-darkness. Max turned on the vessel's exterior lights, illuminating a tunnel stretching ahead. There was something eerie and unwelcoming about the place. Despite the sub's climate-controlled cockpit, Max found himself shivering.

Rivet yelped suddenly. "Shiny gloop, Max!"

Lit by the sub's headlights, Max saw what had got Rivet worked up. The walls were covered in a pale blue, glowing goo. It pulsed slowly with bioluminescence. In a few areas it even criss-crossed the tunnel. Lia had moved ahead on Spike, weaving in and out of the obstacles.

"Better not touch that stuff," said Max. "Whatever it is."

"Don't worry," replied Lia, keeping well away from the walls.

"Where did these tunnels come from?" asked Max. "Could they have been formed by erosion?"

"They're too regular," said Lia. "They were built by someone."

"Or something," Max added. With a whine, Rivet pressed closer.

They followed the energy reading. The tunnel carried on for several hundred metres before widening out. Here the only light was generated by the glowing goo contained in spherical objects stuck to the tunnel walls. These shapes pulsated gently with the blue glow.

"Are they some kind of lamp?" Max wondered aloud as he peered at the spheres. In the centre of each he saw a darker shape, moving in the blue.

Lia gave a gasp of shock as one of the spheres began to crack and split at the top. "I think they might be—"

"Eggs!" gasped Max.

An insect pushed its way from the egg, using large mandibles to cut its way free.

Max looked at the creature with curiosity.

It was antlike – its body segmented with six spindly legs and wavering antennae. But it was oversized, especially the jaws and the blankly staring eyes. It was as big as Rivet! Max didn't like insects at the best of times, but there was something particularly threatening about this creature.

"What is it?" he asked.

"It's a creeper!" cried Lia. "A kind of sea-ant."

"Well, that is one big ant," said Max, not trying to hide his concern. As more of the eggs began to split open, the first creeper started kicking through the water and wriggling towards them.

"Creepers are just drones," Lia said with some amusement. "Diggers and workers. They're harmless!"

Ten more creepers had hatched and were coming towards the sub now. As Max watched, their legs started kicking harder through the water, mandibles clicking together. He tensed as the first super-ant leaped on the sail sub and slashed at the cockpit with its jaws.

"They don't look harmless," he exclaimed. "We're under attack!"

CHAPTER TWO

CREEPER ATTACK

The sail sub rocked violently under the insects' attack. More of the creepers were piling on top, their armoured legs and mandibles smashing the hull. Rivet barked madly at them.

"Easy, boy," said Max, watching the insects swarming over the window. "The cockpit can withstand more than this."

At least I hope it can, he thought to himself.

He tried hitting the throttle to shake them

loose. The sub engines whined and the vehicle shuddered, but it was no use. The creepers sitting on top of the submarine were weighing it down and there was a thud as the sub hit the bottom of the tunnel. They were going nowhere fast. Through the mass of ants covering the window, Max saw that the

creepers were only interested in attacking the sub. They were paying little or no attention to Lia and Spike.

"Lia!" Max said into his headset. "See if you can communicate with them using your Aqua Powers!"

He watched Lia put her fingers to her temples. A frown wrinkled her forehead as she strained to make contact.

"It's no use!" said Lia, throwing up her hands in frustration. "I can't get through to them."

One of the creepers made a violent lunge at the cockpit window, jaws scraping the surface. Max saw with relief that, for the moment the plexiglass seemed to be holding.

"Then why are they attacking?" he asked. "We haven't done anything to them."

"Perhaps they just don't like strangers," said Lia. "We are trespassing in their giant crystal mountain, after all."

"Or they're being controlled by Iris," added Max.

He scanned for the telltale signs of implant control devices on the heads of the creepers, but saw no flashing microchips. Perhaps Lia was right. These creatures could be naturally hostile to anything that invaded their territory.

"Oh, yuck!" Lia exclaimed through Max's headset.

The creepers had started spitting a dark brown resin from their jaws, covering the clear water shield of the cockpit. In seconds it had covered most of the glass.

"Can't see, Max!" barked Rivet.

Max grabbed the lever to open the cockpit and pulled hard in an effort to shake their attackers loose. The mechanism ground horribly, but the canopy didn't budge. *The creepers have sealed it shut with the resin!* Max realised. *We're trapped!*

Just then one of the ants was ripped away from the outside of the cockpit. Spike! Max grinned as he saw the swordfish attack another of the creepers, slashing it away from the sub with his sword.

As another of the creepers fell away, Lia leaped in, the coral spear flashing in her hands. She hacked at creepers left and right, driving them back.

"Turn off the sub lights!" Lia said breathlessly as she continued her attack.

Max knew exactly what she was thinking. The creepers are attracted to the sub's lights! He hit the control console, sending the sub into low power mode. Darkness flooded the cockpit as the lights went out.

Max watched the creepers that hadn't been prised away by Lia and Spike's attacks immediately lose interest in the sub. They started to drift back towards the glowing blue walls of the tunnel.

"You were right, Lia!" said Max. "They were just attracted by the lights!"

He tried pulling the cockpit lever once more. But even without the weight of the attached creepers, the mechanism was stuck fast by the resin.

Max moved to the back of the cockpit and opened the emergency hatch. Water flooded the sub and his gills kicked into action. He swam out towards Lia so he could inspect the sub.

"There doesn't seem to be any major damage," he said as he glanced over the sub. "But we'll need to get that resin off the hull."

"And the moment you power up the sub, those creepers are going to attack again," added Lia.

Max nodded and eyed the sea-ants warily. They had retreated to the walls again and were swarming around the opened eggs.

Just then, Rivet swam out of the sub, his nose lamp glowing bright in the darkness of the tunnel. The effect on the creepers was immediate. They began to scurry along the walls towards the dogbot.

"Turn off your lights, Riv!" said Max.

"Nasty ants!" barked the dogbot, swimming in tight circles to avoid them.

Watching the creepers mindlessly following Rivet gave Max a better idea. "Cancel that last order, Rivet," he said. "Leave your lights on and draw the ants towards you."

"Yes, Max!"

The dogbot began to circle more widely, and the ants followed him around. Then he darted back down the tunnel, forcing them together. With a series of wild electronic barks, he started to herd them into a tight group.

"Go, Rivet!" cried Lia.

Max grinned. "I always wondered if Rivet would be good at herding fish."

Now Rivet had the creepers contained in one section of the tunnel. "Rivet, use your fishing net on them," said Max.

"Okay, Max!"

Rivet fired the net from the compartment

in his belly. The net – made by Max from leftover sail sub alloy – was incredibly strong, yet very flexible. It opened above the tight group of creepers and covered them.

"Good job, boy!" said Max, leaping in to draw the net tight around the trapped insects. They struggled wildly inside, but could not break through the alloy netting. Rivet barked and did a backflip.

"This should hold them," Max said as he rolled the squirming bundle towards the blue goo on the walls. It stuck fast.

With the creepers taken care of, he turned his attention back to the sail sub. "Rivet, lend me some light!" he said.

"Yes, Max!" The dogbot swam over and shone his snout lamp, illuminating the sub. It was in a bad way. The entire outer hull was covered in creeper resin.

Max extracted a cutting tool from the sub's

utility box and started to chip away at the resin. It was tough, but a small shard of the hardened resin came away with some effort. Max caught the shard as it floated away. Max held it up in Rivet's snout lights. The brown resin had turned transparent now that it had hardened. In fact, it gleamed in the light.

"Like crystal," said Lia.

A cold chill went through Max. *Just like the surface of the mountain!* he realised. *This whole place must be a creeper nest!*

Not wasting another second, he swam into the cockpit and performed a wider scan of the area. It revealed a network of tunnels and caverns within the mountain going deep into the seabed. The place was a labyrinth.

"We're inside the creeper colony," said Max. A terrible thought occurred to him as he looked at the squirming mass of trapped creepers. "If those ones were newly hatched, what are the adults like?"

"They're sure to be bigger," said Lia. "Much bigger."

"I was afraid you were going to say that," said Max, as the energy tracker on his wrist started flashing more brightly.

Max studied the tracker carefully. The pings indicated a massive energy reading… closing in by the minute.

He leaped to the control console and charged the torpedoes.

"The Robobeast is here!" he said. "Everyone get ready for battle!"

CHAPTER THREE

CREEPER QUEEN

Max scanned the tunnel ahead, looking for any sign of movement, finger poised on the fire button. The sub was resting on the bottom of the tunnel, but its torpedoes were pointing directly towards the oncoming energy source.

If the Robobeast charges us now, I'm going to throw everything we have at it, thought Max. He had the terrible sense they were being watched by something out there.

Lia floated with her coral spear held high, tensed for battle. Rivet hovered nearby, nose light scanning the tunnel ahead. Nothing!

Max shook his head. *Where is it?* The energy reading showed that the Robobeast should be directly in front of them.

For the briefest instant he saw the water ahead wavering... He almost jabbed his finger down on the fire button... But then the tunnel ahead was still again. Max took a breath.

Getting spooked too easily, he thought. *There's nothing there.*

"The Robobeast must be below us in another tunnel," he said. "That's why we're picking up the reading."

Lia nodded. "So we need to go deeper into the tunnels."

"Deeper into the nest," said Max, heart beating faster.

Powering down the sail sub's systems, Max swam out of the emergency hatch and floated down the tunnel. Once again he had the feeling they were being watched by something…but there was nothing there. He shook it off.

"Too bad we can't take the sub," he said. "But the creepers will be attracted by its lights." He looked at Rivet. "Better keep your nose dimmed as well."

"Yes, Max!"

They started forward, guided by the sinister blue glow of the goo-covered walls. The tunnels angled down, drawing them deeper and deeper into the mountain.

Riding Spike, Lia pointed out more eggs stuck to the tunnel walls. Many of them were ripped open, having already hatched.

"How many creepers are there in this place?" she said.

"It's a massive nest," replied Max.

The passageway joined a much larger tunnel with many smaller ones leading into it. Here the walls glowed bright with many creeper eggs.

"Wait!" cried Max as Lia was about to dart forward on Spike.

The main tunnel was also filled with hundreds of creepers swimming in long lines.

Hiding in the darkness of the smaller tunnel beside Lia, Max saw that there were two distinct types of ant. The majority were black-shelled and very much like the babies that had attacked earlier, although double the size. Max thought these must be adult worker drones.

Then there were even larger ones. These had heavily armoured bodies, tinted deep red. Their pincers were massive and serrated along the inside. They floated along on the edges of the lines of worker ants.

"Soldiers," whispered Lia, pointing to one of the big creepers. "They protect the drones."

"And I thought the small ones were mean-looking," said Max. "But they're all leaving the colony. Where could they be going?"

Lia shrugged. "Not sure... But if there's a Robobeast in here, perhaps Iris has something to do with it."

Max checked the energy tracker. The element's signal was still directly below them, which meant that the Robobeast was waiting for them in the depths of the nest. *What will this one look like?* he wondered. *A giant metal creeper?* He shuddered at the thought.

Leading the way forward again, Max swam down behind the cover of craggy rocks at the side of the main tunnel. He moved stealthily. When he reached gaps in the rock cover, he stopped and checked that no creepers were nearby before leading the others on. *Those ants mustn't know we're here,* he thought as he led the way forward slowly.

The main tunnel finally widened out into a massive chamber full of creepers. They swarmed over the domed ceiling of the cavern – thousands of them. More hatched from eggs even as they watched. The full-grown ones joined the lines flowing out of the colony in a never-ending stream.

"They're blocking our way to the element," said Max, holding up the energy tracker. The signal was coming from directly below the chamber. "Any ideas on how we can get by them?"

"Run for it, Max!" Rivet suggested, his tail spinning enthusiastically.

Max grinned at his loyal dogbot. *Maybe that's not such a bad idea.* If they were fast, perhaps they could make the other side of the chamber before the creepers even noticed.

"It's not that simple," said Lia, clearly guessing what he was thinking. "Up there!"

Max looked towards where she was pointing. High up in the top of the cavern, a ledge of crystalline resin jutted out. From this vantage point a creeper with purple armour, three times the size of one of the red ants watched the scene below. Her mandibles snapped together, producing a series of clicking noises that echoed throughout the chamber. The workers responded to these clicks, as if receiving orders.

It's the creeper queen! Max realised. "She's controlling the entire colony from up there."

"And look!" exclaimed Lia. "On her head!"

Max followed her gaze and saw what Lia was talking about. A computer chip the size of a man's hand was attached to the bulbous

head of the creeper queen. A red light blinked rapidly as she scanned the endless rows of ants. One of Iris's microchip implants!

"Iris is controlling the queen!" said Max.

"And the queen controls the whole colony," added Lia.

They looked at one another with terrible realisation. With the queen under her power, Iris could control thousands…maybe millions of creeper ants.

Max looked back at the terrible scene before them and thought of his home city. "It's an army," he said quietly. "So this is how Iris is planning to destroy Aquora."

CHAPTER FOUR

STEALTH MISSION

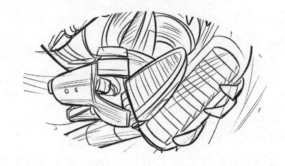

"We need to target the creeper queen," said Max. "If we remove that chip, Iris will lose control of the colony. Then we can walk right past the creepers to get the element, providing the Robobeast doesn't get in the way."

Lia looked sceptical. "And how are you going to get the chip? Walk up there and grab it off the queen's head?"

Max thought for a moment. His eyes fell

on Rivet and he snapped his fingers. *Got it! The in-built Electromagnetic Pulse!*

"I can use Rivet's EMP to disable the chip," he said. "It will deactivate any electronic devices."

"You'll still need to get in range," said Lia. "And that's going to be close enough for those soldiers to see you coming."

"Not if we're camouflaged," said Max. He cautiously put his fingers into the goo and scooped up a handful. Then he smeared it across Rivet's back.

"Yuck, Max!" yapped the dogbot.

"It's just so we can blend in with the walls, Rivet," said Max as he spread more of it on his own arms and neck. "It will come off… I hope."

Lia stepped forward. "I'm coming too."

"You should hang back here with Spike," he said. "Riv and I will be less noticeable on our own. We mustn't be seen until the very last moment."

Lia looked like she was about to argue, but then she nodded. "Okay. But be careful."

"We will be," said Max.

He and Rivet set off along the side of the cavern, keeping close to the walls. Suddenly one of the soldier ants appeared directly ahead, its mandibles clicking together. Max froze, pressing himself against the wall. For a moment it seemed that the ant was looking right at him, about to attack…but then it passed on by, close enough that its leg almost brushed his body.

It's working! Max thought with relief. Maybe their eyesight isn't so good after all.

Halfway along the cavern wall they stopped, directly below the ledge upon which the creeper queen perched. Her giant antennae flicked this way and that, large and powerful enough to create a current that Max could feel pushing against his body. He kicked up with powerful strokes, closely followed by Rivet. Weaving in and out of the creeper eggs, he kept close so the blue goo covering his body gave the best camouflage possible.

"Take it easy, boy," Max whispered to Rivet as they reached the ledge. "We're almost there."

They moved fast and low, stopping to the rear of the queen. Max looked over the insect with wide eyes. Up close she was even larger than he had expected – her head alone was the size of one of the soldier ants. Her body was double the size of the sail sub! The queen's exoskeleton was dark and as thick as the hull of a sub too. Her segmented tail section was elongated and filled with the blue glow of new creeper eggs. Max thought there had to be a hundred unlaid eggs inside the queen.

Rivet gave a low growl.

"Shhh!" said Max. Glancing round the body of the queen, he saw that she was still intently watching the procession of creepers out of the colony. The control chip blinked on the side of her head.

Let's knock out this chip and get out of here, Max thought.

Opening a compartment on Rivet's side, he brought the EMP online. A button flashed, indicating that the charge was ready for deployment.

"Max, watch out!" Lia cried through his headset.

He looked up in time to see the giant shape of the creeper queen spinning round. *She's seen us!*

Before Max could activate the EMP, one of the queen's armoured legs shot out towards

him. It hit him square in the chest. Max flew
back along the ledge and landed hard on his
back, pain jolting his spine. Rivet leaped at
the queen, but she swatted him away with
another of her legs. Then she advanced on
Max. He backed away. More soldier ants
were moving in on his position from all

directions. Max saw that they were trying to surround him.

The creeper queen lunged again, snapping with her mandibles. Max rolled forward, under her body, drawing his hyperblade as he did so. With a thrust, he jabbed at the queen's exposed underside.

The blade bounced harmlessly off the thick exoskeleton, but the queen leaped back, keeping her egg-laden section away from him. As she retreated along the ledge, Max turned his attention to Rivet. Five soldier ants were attacking, trying to pin him down with their legs and tear him apart with their jaws. Rivet fought hard – barking and biting at them – but he was outnumbered and outsized by his attackers.

"Hold on, boy!" yelled Max, leaping forward with his blade raised.

He slashed at one of the creepers attacking

Rivet. The hyperblade bounced off the ant's head and it leaped back, although there seemed to be little damage to its thick shell. Max pulled his blaster with his free hand and fired a couple of bolts at another charging creeper. The insect stopped momentarily, but then continued on the attack once more.

I'm not even scratching their armour! Max thought. At his side Rivet was fighting madly as well, metal jaws locked around the leg of one of the soldiers.

Fighting back another wave of creepers, Max saw the queen rise from the platform and swim away, flanked by more soldiers. *Of course she won't fight us directly,* Max realised. *She has an army to do that!* His heart sank as he saw their chance to get Iris's control chip swimming into the distance.

The snapping jaws of one of the soldiers reminded Max that they were completely surrounded, and more were coming in for the attack! He brought his blaster round to hit an attacking creeper. Too late. It hit him with full force. Max flew back, the blaster tumbling from his grasp. The leg of another ant swiped the back of his knees and he crashed against the ledge with a cry of pain. The creeper reared above Max, mandibles poised to strike down at his exposed chest...

"Get off him!"

The point of Lia's coral spear glanced off the head of the creeper as she charged in on Spike. As the stunned ant went down, Max rolled to safety, bringing his hyperblade up. There was a whoosh of water around him as Spike raced by in a protective circle, forcing the soldiers back.

"Thanks, you two!" Max said. "That one almost had me!"

"There are too many of them!" cried Lia as

she continued to jab at the soldiers with her spear. "What do we do?"

"We need to regroup and work out how to get that chip," said Max. "Where's Rivet?"

As if to answer his question, there was a high-pitched bark from the middle of the chamber.

"Help, Max!"

One of the soldiers had locked its limbs around Rivet. The dogbot was swimming in desperate circles in an effort to shake it loose, moving further away and closer into the swarm of creepers flooding the chamber.

"No!" cried Max as he saw the creeper starting to cut through the side of Rivet's titanium alloy body with its jaws.

Max swam directly at an approaching creeper. Twisting up at the last moment, he kicked off the ant's head towards the middle of the chamber…hyperblade at the ready…

"Rivet! I'm coming!"

CHAPTER FIVE

IRIS TALKS

Max swam up fast on the creeper attacking Rivet. He raised his hyperblade to strike…but the dogbot was whizzing around so fast that he couldn't land a strike.

Max turned to Lia. "My blaster!"

She raced toward the ledge. Scooping up the blaster, she dropped it over the side towards him. "Catch!"

The blaster arced through the water painfully slowly. Max kicked up to meet it…

closed his fingers around the grip…and spun in the direction of Rivet and the attacking creeper.

Steady, he told himself as he looked down the sights at the fast-moving target.

The pair was coming around again, the creeper was now snapping at Rivet's tail with its jaws. Max kept his arm level and aimed for where they were going to be. He held his breath as he squeezed the trigger…

WHAM!

The blast hit the creeper's midsection. Its legs flailed and it fell away. Finally free, Rivet propelled his way towards him.

"Thanks, Max!"

Max was already turning to face the other soldiers. *The fight isn't over yet…*

But he was surprised to see that, instead of swarming them, the soldier ants were moving away across the chamber. Lia rode up on Spike, looking just as confused.

"The soldiers are backing off!" she said. "But why?"

Max shrugged. "Perhaps they got spooked by my blaster skills."

"All hundred of them?" she said with a wry smile.

He holstered the pistol. "Well, maybe not all of them."

A shimmering patch of water began to rise from a passageway in the bottom of the cavern. Max recognised it instantly and tensed for action. He'd seen the same shimmer from the sail sub when they first picked up the Robobeast's energy reading.

The distortion in the water intensified. A new Robobeast materialised in the chamber right before them! Max gasped. This one was clearly modelled on a creature whose appearance could strike fear into the hearts

of the most experienced seafarer.

"A goblin shark," he said under his breath.

Its fully robotic body was long and sleek, made of reflective steel. Energy weapons stuck out from both sides of the shark near its fins, with a larger one mounted on its dorsal. The Robobeast's body ended in an elongated snout that was sharply pointed, perhaps for use as a ram. Beneath this nose section was a

pair of dead black eyes. Its mouth drew back to reveal two rows of razor-sharp metal teeth, almost in a grin. This leering expression seemed to mock them.

Max swallowed heavily. "Not pretty," he said, staring up at it.

"It wasn't your blaster those soldiers were running from!" exclaimed Lia. She was trying and failing to disguise the quaver in her voice.

"They don't need to fight. The Robobeast can do that!"

Max nodded. "It must be using the Blinc to power a cloaking device. It was watching us earlier in the tunnel!"

He shuddered at the thought of that grinning face studying them, hidden by the invisibility field. It could have struck at any time, but it had waited for its moment to reveal itself. Clearly Iris had something more in store for them than simple destruction…she could have achieved that with the creepers alone.

Even as Max was thinking it, a small metal capsule whizzed into sight from behind the goblin shark. "Iris!"

"I thought her plasmagram capsule was destroyed by your bomb," said Lia.

"So did I," said Max.

Liquid metal oozed from the capsule, forming into the image of a twelve-year-old girl. The metal husk rested in the middle of her waist, like a belt buckle, its controlled magnetic field holding the plasma in place.

"The damage to my capsule was easily fixable," Iris said, dismissively. Her face showed no sign of emotion, but as she looked over Max and his friends the image glowed a deeper blue. "I'd like you to meet Mirroc."

Max gritted his teeth. "What do you want, Iris?"

"My directives are simple," she replied, eyes sparkling. "I must identify and eradicate threats to the starship *Liberty*. I have identified you and your people as a threat and you will be eradicated. Please provide me with the coordinates to your city, Aquora."

"I don't think so," said Max, springing toward the plasmagram.

Lia placed a restraining hand on his arm. "Easy, Max!" she whispered. "Remember those eye lasers."

Taking another deep breath, Max nodded. He turned his attention back to Iris and said, "You'll never get those coordinates from me."

Iris tilted her head to one side, studying him. "Objectives have now changed." Her image flashed bright red.

What? thought Max.

A pair of energy beams shot from Iris's eyes, straight at Max. He flung himself out the way, but Iris tracked him with her gaze, and with another zap, two more laser beams streaked towards him.

"Max, watch out!" Lia called.

Off balance, Max couldn't dodge. Desperately, he drew his hyperblade and swung it in front of his eyes. The bolts of energy bounced off the vernium blade, as

pain exploded through his arm. The force sent him flying through the water, crumpling against the cavern wall.

"Mirroc, finish them," said Iris. The plasmagram withdrew into the capsule, which shot away through the water and disappeared into a tunnel.

The massive Robobeast stared hungrily at Max. It thrashed its tail, shimmered...and disappeared.

Max felt a mighty rush of water towards him, the only clue he had that Mirroc was charging. Summoning his remaining strength, he kicked to one side. The invisible body of the robotic goblin shark rushed by, pushing a swell of water in its wake. And then it was gone.

Lia rushed to his side. "Where is it?" she said, looking around in all directions.

Max scanned the chamber as well, but

saw nothing. Fully cloaked, Mirroc could be anywhere.

"What do we do?" said Lia.

"Swim out of the nest!" replied Max. "I'll get out of here on Rivet!"

Lia turned Spike and sent him speeding out of the cavern in the direction they'd come. Max looked around for Rivet. He knew that holding on to the dogbot would be his fastest way out of the nest.

But Rivet was swimming in circles in the middle of the cavern. He seemed confused, as if he'd forgotten where he was and didn't know which way to go.

"Can't swim, Max!" he cried as his master swam over.

"Slow down, boy!" said Max, catching hold of the dogbot and bringing him to a halt. "Easy!"

Only too aware that Mirroc might strike

again from any direction, Max ran his hands over Rivet's body. There were scratches from where the creeper had slashed at him, but no serious damage. Then he saw the problem.

The last notch of Rivet's tail was missing. His navigation system was gone! This was why he was swimming in circles. *It must have come loose when the creepers attacked Rivet,* thought Max. He scanned the floor of the cavern, but couldn't see the nav chip.

A rush of water from directly above cut through Max's thoughts. He looked up and saw a swirling vortex of water rushing down on him with terrible speed.

Mirroc was coming!

CHAPTER SIX

FIGHT AND FLIGHT

With a sharp kick, Max sent himself arcing backwards through the water. Just in time! The gaping, tooth-filled jaws of the goblin shark flashed into visibility and clamped shut right where he had been a split second before.

The Robobeast hurtled past, carried by its own momentum. Its wake hit Max full force, sending him spinning backwards. As he fought to right himself, Max saw the pointed nose of the shark smash into the wall, sending a shock wave through the whole cavern. The walls shook and lumps of rock fell through the water. The Robobeast twisted violently. It was thrashing around aimlessly, jaws snapping and its great eyes rolling white.

"I think that made it mad!" cried Max as he pushed himself away from the churning water around the beast. He knew that Mirroc would be on the attack again any second, but for the moment he was even more worried about how he was going to get Rivet out of the collapsing cavern.

Lia appeared at his side on Spike. "Let's get out of here!"

Max saw that she had guided Rivet over, one hand placed behind his head. The unhappy dogbot was looking around wildly, totally confused without his navigation chip. Max grabbed Rivet's paw and gave Lia a nod.

"Quick!" he said. "That shark is going to be on us again any second!"

Lia sent Spike racing away and Max pointed Rivet after her.

"Follow Spike, Rivet!"

The dogbot's propeller whirred and he set off in pursuit, guided by his master. Max didn't look back, focussing on the entrance of the glowing tunnel that would send them back towards the surface. But behind them he

could feel the terrible onrush of something very large...

Mirroc in pursuit.

The tunnels were clear of creepers now, at least. Max and his friends flew down the narrow tunnels, twisting this way and that.

This place really is a maze! thought Max as they took a right at high speed, into a tunnel almost identical to so many they'd passed.

WHAM!

The tunnel walls shook massively from a collision. Max glanced over his shoulder and saw the pointed, battering-ram nose of Mirroc coming up fast again...

WHAM!

It smashed into the wall as they whizzed past. The Robobeast's teeth gnashed. Its whole body thrashed in rage, sending shock waves through the confined area of the tunnels. But it kept on coming. Its bulk filled the tunnel behind them completely... A steel wall of razor teeth and battering ram coming closer and closer...

"Give it all you've got, Rivet!" cried Max as they took a left into another tunnel.

The dogbot's propeller whirred madly and they put some precious metres between them and their pursuer.

"I hope this is the right way!" shouted Lia as she drove Spike forward.

Max didn't want to consider they might have taken a wrong turn, or that they might be headed towards a dead end tunnel. It would mean certain destruction.

VUH-DOOOOOM!

An electric hum was audible even above the gnashing and panting of the Robobeast. Max knew the sound of a weapons system coming online when he heard one. Mirroc was powering up his energy cannons!

"Get ready to move!" he shouted to Lia, seeing the blue electricity at the shark's raised tail growing in intensity…powering up for a blast… "Now!"

Max sent Rivet careening right so hard that they scraped the side of the tunnel. Lia went hard left. An energy bolt screamed past them down the middle of the tunnel. It hit a section of rock. Crystal shards flew in all

directions. Max had no choice but to drive Rivet on through the debris. *Mirroc is going to bring the whole nest down at this rate!* he thought.

"Ouch, Max!" protested the dogbot as a shard ricocheted off his head.

"Faster, boy!" ordered Max. "We're almost out of here!"

THRUMMM! THRUMMM! THRUMMM!

Three more energy bolts fired in quick succession down the tunnel. Max twisted Rivet, sending him into a corkscrew to avoid the blasts. Sections of tunnel exploded all around them, turning the clear water cloudy with dust. *Missed!* Max thought triumphantly as the Robobeast scraped the tunnel wall behind them, snapping at the debris-filled water. Lia was okay too, having raced ahead on Spike.

"Look!" she called back. "Clear ocean!"

Max grinned wildly as he saw the exit to the nest speeding towards them. He silently willed Rivet to move even faster and the dogbot seemed to sense it, surging ahead until a second later…

WHOOSH!

They shot out of the nest and into the open ocean. Max let out a triumphant shout with the relief of being out of the tunnels. Up ahead Lia sent Spike in a wide arc. But it wasn't over yet.

Mirroc exploded from the nest. Its body now showed the marks of where it had thrown itself against the tunnel walls – a network of scratches and dents along its silvered sides.

But the Robobeast just floated before them. Electricity flashed at its tail. The rows of teeth gleamed.

"Why isn't it attacking?" asked Lia.

Max shook his head slowly. He met the shark's lifeless eyes and understood what was happening.

"It's playing with us," he said. "Waiting for the moment for the kill."

As he said this, the Robobeast gave a powerful flick of its tail, charging its energy beam. Max tensed, ready to dodge the blast.

At least we'll have more space to manoeuvre

now we're out of those tunnels.

And then Mirroc disappeared.

"The invisibility cloak!" gasped Lia. "We're sitting ducks!"

"Floating fish, more like!" said Max.

The thrum of energy and a flash of light from above was the only warning they got of the blast. Max pushed Lia out of the way as the energy beam passed between them, just centimetres away. Max thought he could feel his eyebrows singeing. He'd lost his grip on Rivet, who was again spinning wildly.

"Try to make it to those rocks, Rivet!" order Max. "Keep out of sight. You can't help this time!"

"Yes, Max!" barked the dogbot as he spun towards the ocean floor. Lia shot towards the surface on Spike, heading into the sunlight.

VUH-DOOOOOM!

Max felt a surge of adrenaline. The sound

of Mirroc's energy cannons charging up had come from right behind him. He spun round, scanning the waters intently for anything that would betray the location of the Robobeast.

But this time there was no telltale shimmer in the water. If he hadn't heard the cannons for himself, he wouldn't have believed the deadly foe was floating right before him.

This beast is toying with me, Max realised. Without Rivet to get him out of trouble or the protection of the sail sub there was no chance of escape.

Mirroc can destroy me at any second!

CHAPTER SEVEN

RUN FOR COVER

Max twisted his body in a desperate evasive manoeuvre as the energy beams licked the surrounding water. Luckily his reflexes were sharp from many adventures, or he would have been sliced to ribbons for sure. Instead he plunged in a spiral towards the ocean floor.

Got to get to cover!

Making it to the sandy ocean bottom, he half-swam, half-clawed his way to a clump of rocks. And just in time he reached the gap between the sand and stone as Mirroc's backwash whooshed overhead. Suddenly the sea was bright with a barrage of energy blasts released all at once. Sand and rock flew in every direction. Max put his head down and waited for his destruction.

But it didn't come. Max looked up and saw that the jagged rocks overhead were providing just enough cover from Mirroc's attack. There was a bellow from above, the invisible monster showing its rage at not being able to destroy him. *It won't be long, though,* Max thought grimly, looking at his meagre hiding place. *These rocks aren't going to survive many more attacks like that.*

"Coming, Max!" growled Rivet.

Max watched the dogbot burst from his own shelter to help. But Rivet succeeded only in swimming in a wild circle as before, still lost without his navigation chip.

"Stay back, Riv!" yelled Max. A rush of water above them was his warning that the cloaked Robobeast was on the attack again. "You can't do any good like that!"

With a frustrated bark, Rivet pushed himself through the water back to cover as Max's headset crackled.

"We're on our way too!" It was Lia. Max looked up and saw her on Spike, a tiny speck in the distance racing back to help. But he also sensed the approach of Mirroc.

"No, Lia!" warned Max. "It's too dangerous!"

"Like that ever stopped us!" she called back.

Max smiled at his friend's bravery, although he knew that Lia wouldn't make it before Mirroc's next attack. The ocean before him warped with the sign of the cloaked beast. Suddenly out of that distortion came a wall of energy beams, all aimed at the rock he was crouched behind.

Move! Max pushed himself away from his hiding place seconds before the rocks exploded in the latest energy barrage.

The explosion sent shock waves crashing over him, but Max righted himself and fled straight into the dust cloud. For the moment he was invisible to Mirroc. *Good as any cloaking device!*

But Mirroc must have seen him enter, because he swooped through the dust with alarming speed for a beast so large. Completely visible now, the giant, tooth-lined-jaws opened wide, filling Max's vision. With a cry, he threw himself to the side. The jaws snapped shut centimetres from his body and the Robobeast rushed on by. Caught in the terrible wash, Max was sent tumbling and bouncing along the metal body.

Reaching for the holster on his hip, Max drew the blaster and fired off three shots as he spun in Mirroc's wake. The energy bolts lashed the shark's silvered hide.

And then Mirroc was twisting in the ocean and the long, pointed snout was coming right at him like a spear. This time, Max swam

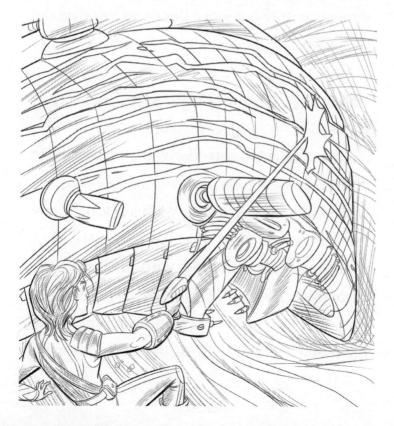

directly towards the Roboshark. As the beast filled his vision, Max swam up. He kicked off Mirroc's nose and somersaulted as the beast passed underneath.

Take this! Max fired off three more blasts. Scorch marks appeared on Mirroc's flanks. Max's heart sank. The blaster had left no damage – nothing more than a smudge on the steel skin.

I'll need more than a blaster to hurt this beast, he thought. Then it came to him. *The sail sub's torpedoes!*

"Max!" It was Lia, flying in to help from above.

"I'm going back to the tunnels for the sail sub!" he cried. "Cover me!"

He tossed her the blaster with all his strength. Swooping in on Spike, Lia reached out a hand and caught it. As Mirroc came in for the attack from above, she was already twisting round to spray the shark with a rapid-fire volley.

"Nice work, Lia!" Max said into his communicator as he powered through the water back towards the mountain entrance. "Try to keep it busy. But don't get eaten!"

Twisting this way and that on Spike, Lia laughed as she peppered Mirroc's snout with more blaster fire. "Don't worry! This brute is too slow for Spike and me!"

I certainly hope so, thought Max as he swam into the darkness of the tunnel entrance once more. He didn't like leaving Lia out there with the Robobeast, but the sail sub was their only hope to bring the creature down.

He saw the squat shape of the sub resting where they'd left it and swam over. Lumps of crystal had fallen from the ceiling, dislodged when Mirroc was charging around, no doubt, and were covering the emergency hatch. Max went to the canopy instead, and pulled

on the plexiglass with all his might. But the cockpit cover was still sealed shut with the hardened resin from the creepers. He pulled again, gritting his teeth with effort. No use!

Lia's voice rang out over his communicator. "Max, watch out! Mirroc's coming straight for you!"

Max moved for the sail sub's emergency hatch. He grabbed one of the fallen pieces of

crystal and heaved it aside. The water in the tunnel rippled as something large entered the nest. *Mirroc!* Max grabbed another piece of crystal and pulled it away from the hatch, which was now clear enough to open. He dived through into the sub.

The auto-system on the vessel kicked in and the cockpit immediately began to drain of water as he entered. Max staggered towards the pilot's seat as air filled the sub from the oxygen tanks. He slammed his hand down on the ignition panel and the engines hummed…warming up…

Come on!

Max watched the shimmer of the Robobeast filling the tunnel entrance. Iris's invisible destroyer was almost upon him.

He leaped into the pilot's seat and pulled back hard on the control stick, even though the engines hummed at half power. Max knew that he had to move fast, before it was too late. The sub began to rise from the bottom of the tunnel.

Faster!

Max pulled back even harder on the stick, willing the sub to rise…

The surge of water that came with Mirroc's approach wave hit the sub with incredible force, buffeting it back.

The Robobeast was going to crush the sub with Max in it!

CHAPTER EIGHT

TO CATCH A FISH

With a desperate cry, Max jammed his fist down on the sub's turbo button. The thrusters fired. The sub lurched forward, throwing Max back across the cockpit. Mirroc shot past, buffeting the vehicle and sending it off course. The tunnel shook as the shark's battering nose slammed into the crystal walls.

Max brought the sub round at full speed towards the tunnel exit. Seconds later it shot out into the ocean. He allowed himself a relieved breath at having the sub in open water again, and out of the creeper labyrinth. But his heart was still pumping hard and his fingers clenched the controls.

Mirroc can attack any second, he thought, turning the sub around. *Let's sink this beast.*

The tunnel entrance was in his sights and there was no sign of Mirroc, but Max didn't trust his eyes. The shark could be cloaked and lying in wait. But he wasn't going to give the Robobeast the chance to attack. Max jabbed his finger on the torpedo fire button three times in quick succession.

Torpedoes streaked away from the sub in the direction of the tunnel. They hit with a series of muffled explosions all around the entrance. Crystal shattered all around, swallowing the opening.

As the dust cleared, Max stared at the

blocked opening, hardly daring to breathe. He looked at Lia, floating on Spike. She gave him the slightest of smiles.

Lia said, "Do you think—"

A gigantic mass smashed through the crystal debris covering the opening. With the force of the impact, Mirroc's cloak failed for the briefest moment and the

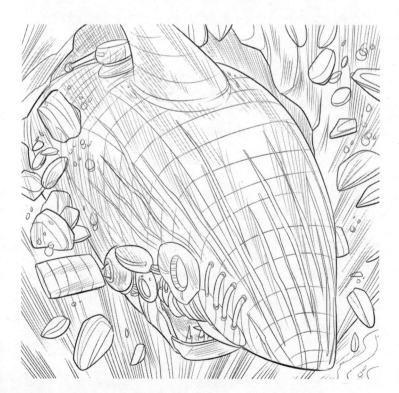

Robobeast became fully visible.

It didn't work! thought Max as he watched Mirroc heading straight for Lia and Spike.

"Watch out!" Max cried into his communicator.

The warning gave Lia just enough time to send Spike dodging away as Mirroc unleashed a series of energy blasts in their direction. They narrowly evaded the deadly beam and flew out of danger.

"How can we beat an invisible enemy?" Lia asked as she reined Spike in.

Max shook his head. "I don't know."

He looked back at the direction from which the beams had come. Mirroc was thrashing around for the moment, focused on dislodging the crystal debris that was covering its back.

Suddenly it came to Max...

"We can't beat an invisible enemy," he said.

"So, what?" asked Lia. "We just run away?"

"No," said Max. "We're going to throw some light on this problem. Lia, try to keep Mirroc busy while I go for the tunnel again."

"You're going back in there?"

"I need to get some of that glowing goo," he replied. "Just keep it occupied!"

"Come on, Spike!" said Lia. She sent the swordfish towards an area of wavering water where Mirroc lay in wait, her coral spear raised. With a cry, she jabbed the spear at the shimmering water. Mirroc gave a great howl and energy beams flew. Lia was already darting away on her nimble swordfish.

Max sent the sub back towards the shattered tunnel entrance.

As the sub passed into the tunnel, Max worked the control panel. He adjusted the super-flexible sails so the cone twisted on its side, forming a kind of scoop. Then he steered the sub close to the walls. The scoop made

contact with a grinding judder. Glowing goo began to collect in the sail.

It's working!

When he had collected as much gloop as he dared without damaging the sail, Max sent the sub whizzing back out of the tunnel. Outside, he saw that Mirroc was directing energy blasts at Spike and Lia, trying to bring them down. But the swordfish was proving too fast and agile to be hit.

"Hold on, Lia!" said Max. "I'm coming!"

"Whatever you're going to do, make it fast!" she cried. "Spike's getting tired!"

Max put the sub into a climb, making sure that the gloop he had collected in the sail did not spill. He guided the vessel above the spot in the ocean where Lia and Spike were twisting this way and that, evading the attack of Mirroc.

"Bring Mirroc under the sub!" ordered Max. "I've got a present for him."

Lia sighed. "Do you always have to use me as bait?"

Before Max could reply, she was already sending Spike zooming towards the area under the sub. Energy blasts flew around her, but she zigzagged this way and that, anticipating every attack. As the shimmer of Mirroc approached, she guided Spike upwards towards the sub.

"This is our only chance!" she cried. "Don't miss!"

Max gritted his teeth. "I won't."

The waters below the sub shimmered. Max poised his hand over the sail sub console. The shimmer grew closer...

Got to get this right.

Closer.

"Now, Lia! Go under the sub!" he shouted.

She zoomed beneath the vessel on Spike.

Got you, Mirroc! thought Max.

He hit the sail release button. As the scoop collapsed, the collected blue goo spilled through the water. The goo splattered across the cloaked body of Mirroc, tracing the sleek lines of its back and fins.

The Robobeast twisted frantically in the water. Lumps of goo flew away as it writhed, but the body was visible enough now. Goo had poured over the Robobeast's nose and jaws. Semi-visible teeth glowed in the water. If anything, Mirroc looked even more fearsome in this half-revealed state.

You are *ugly,* thought Max as the shark stopped twisting and turned its leering face towards him. *Even by the standards of Iris's monsters.*

"Good work, Max!" said Lia, cutting through his thoughts. "Now can we blow this thing up and get out of here?"

Max nodded as he powered up the torpedoes once more. "Yeah. Mustn't damage the Blinc, though." He looked at the flashing object in the beast's forehead and locked the torpedoes on the tail section.

As if sensing the danger, Mirroc flexed its

mighty body in readiness for a final charge.

"Fine!" Lia said. "Just blow it up a little! But do it…"

Mirroc shot forward with alarming speed, jaws opening wide to consume the sail sub.

"Now!"

Max hit the FIRE button.

CHAPTER NINE

BLAST OFF

The torpedoes flew straight and true towards a section of Mirroc's flank.

Come on! Max willed the missiles to hit home.

Then Mirroc reacted. He turned his gaping maw towards the path of the torpedoes.

Oh dear, thought Max.

The missiles flew into the mouth of Mirroc and were swallowed by the blackness.

"Lia, watch out!" Max yelled…

As there was a muffled explosion and a

flash from deep within the Robobeast. The robotic goblin shark ruptured along its sides, spilling fire into the ocean. Shards of metal, components and broken teeth shot out of the explosion at high speed.

Max pulled hard on the steering column,

sending the sail sub away from the blast. Shrapnel peppered the hull. Once he was out of range of the blast, Max looked back at the remains of Iris's third monster. With the beast's cloaking device destroyed, their foe was fully visible. Mirroc was a broken shell, floating towards the bottom of the ocean. A single black eye stared back at Max, and then closed forever.

"You did it, Max!" cried Lia, coming in on Spike.

"What about the Blinc?" said Max, scanning the wreckage of the Robobeast. His heart leaped as he saw something flash amidst the wreckage coming to rest on the seabed. "There it is!"

Lia raced down to the wreck. Weaving between jagged pieces of Mirroc's carcass, she found the battery pack and carefully pulled it free. Max watched, breath held, as she looked over the pack with care. Finally, she held it up triumphantly for him to see.

"It's undamaged!" she said.

Max laughed with relief. Mirroc was nothing more than scrap metal. The Blinc was rescued. *We've won!*

A robotic bark sounded in Max's communicator and he remembered Rivet. Steering the sail sub down to the rocks where the dogbot was hiding, he opened the emergency hatch.

"In you get, boy!" he called.

Rivet moved clumsily from the rocks. Max helped the dogbot inside the sub. Rivet wagged his tail and nuzzled Max's arm as he lay dripping on the floor.

"Bad shark gone, Max?"

Max nodded. "Yes, Riv. Bad shark gone." He reached for his toolbox and opened the hatch on Rivet's back. "Now, let's see what we can do about your navigation system."

There was a spare chip in the toolbox and Max set to work attaching this to Rivet's motherboard with a screwdriver and soldering iron. With the chip installed, Max closed the hatch and nodded to his dog.

"Give it a try."

The dogbot got to his feet and tried turning in a circle. He managed, but was still clumsy, bumping into the side of the sub.

"Feel woozy, Max!" he protested.

"Just take it slow," said Max. "That spare chip isn't as high tech as you're used to. But it will have to do until we can get your tail beacon back."

Rivet nodded and tried another spin, a little more gracefully this time. "Better, Max!"

Max patted him on the head and took the sub controls again, steering over to where Lia was still holding Mirroc's battery pack.

Swimming out through the airlock he went to join her.

"Are you okay?" he asked.

"Fine," she said, stroking Spike's flank. "We both are. Mirroc was some Robobeast, though."

Max nodded, looking back at the twisted remains of the goblin shark. The dust was settling around it. "Not any more," he said. "Just another piece of wreckage at the bottom of the ocean now. Iris will be disappointed."

Max took the battery pack from Lia and swam with it back into the sub. At the console he used his tools to strip away the outer casing of the battery to reveal the Blinc. The translucent liquid shone in the centre of the pack.

He retrieved the special four-compartment container from a drawer. Max opened a third and then set to work on opening the central

section of the battery from Mirroc. With great care, he poured the Blinc from the pack into the safety of the container and sealed it up tightly.

Three of the four elements, he thought, inspecting the container. *Only one more to rescue and then we can head back to Aquora, restart the generators, and save everyone from chaos and dehydration.*

"Max!" cried Lia, pointing into the

distance. "The creepers!"

He saw the trail of insects marching across the ocean floor as far as the eye could see, heads down as if following a silent command. *Where are they going?* Max wondered.

"Let's follow them," he said, steering the sub round and firing the thrusters.

They caught up with the line of ants and followed it, Lia keeping pace with the sub on Spike. For their part, the creepers seemed unaware of their presence. They were focused solely on their task – their destination, whatever it was. Max checked his energy tracker and detected a massive reading up ahead – the place where the creepers were congregating. Something was going on there, something big.

"We've been here before," said Lia as they raced ahead. "We're headed for the wreck of the SS *Liberty*!"

"And so are the creepers," said Max, grimly.

The wreck of the massive starship loomed in the distance, a dark mass at first, becoming more distinct as they approached.

And as Max grew closer he saw the lines of ants ending at the *Liberty* and crawling up the sides of the giant vessel. In fact, the starship was swarming with creepers! There were thousands of them, moving this way and that over the hull. The larger, soldier ants, had formed a protective circle around the wreck – ready to repel anyone who tried to stop the workers from their tasks.

"So many of them!" Lia gasped.

Max watched a group of creepers spraying resin into a damaged section of hull. In other areas the resin had hardened already, forming a protective shell. "They're patching up the *Liberty*!" he said.

"You're right!" said Lia. "It looks like

they're making it watertight."

But why? wondered Max. *The* Liberty *is a wreck.*

Lights began to come on along the length of the ship, illuminating the ocean for kilometres in every direction. A deep *whup-whup-whup* resonated through the water, becoming more intense.

"What's that?" asked Lia.

"It sounds like fusion engines powering up," replied Max.

"You mean Iris is going to fly the ship out of here?" said Lia.

Max stared on in disbelief as the creepers finished sealing the hull. Their repair job was complete. The ship shifted on the seabed, starting to rise from the spot where it had lain for centuries.

"The final element," he said. "Iris must be using it to power the entire ship. We've got to stop her from leaving."

He worked his fingers across the console, aiming torpedoes at the *Liberty*.

Fire!

Torpedoes streaked through the water and slammed into the side of the ship seconds later. Creepers flew in all directions, but as the bubbles cleared, the hull was untouched. With a powerful roar of its engines, the SS *Liberty* turned so that its torpedo tubes were pointing directly at them.

"Max! Watch out!" cried Lia.

A volley of high-power energy blasts flew at them as they dodged this way and that. One of them scraped the sail sub, sending it spinning wildly. *A direct hit from one of those would finish us,* he thought, preparing to evade another attack.

But it didn't come…

The SS *Liberty* instead turned in the

opposite direction. Three massive, circular
exhausts flashed bright blue with power. And
then the ship started moving away with the
creeper army still clinging to its hull, picking
up speed by the second.

"Where are they going?" asked Lia as she

rode up on Spike.

"Rivet's navigation chip!" said Max, a cold chill going through him. "Iris knows the location of Aquora now."

Lia gave a horrified gasp. "And that's where she's taking the creeper army! Without power, the city is defenceless!"

"No!" cried Max, imagining the ship reaching his home city…the creepers swarming out of the sea and attacking his people at their most vulnerable.

With another cry, he fired off two more torpedoes after the *Liberty*, but the ship was already growing small in the distance, easily out of range. Max put the sail sub to full power and set off in pursuit.

"We have to catch them!" he said. "We're the only ones who can save Aquora!"

Lia was right beside the sub. "So we've got to take on Iris, a starship, and an army of creepers. Sounds like a tough one, even for us."

Max nodded at her through the cockpit window. "If anyone can do it, we can!"

I'm not stopping until my home is safe from that insane computer once and for all, he thought.

Max pushed the sub to its limit in pursuit of their enemy and shouted, "Full steam ahead!"

Don't miss Max's next Sea Quest adventure,
when he faces

BLISTRA
THE SEA DRAGON

COLLECT ALL THE BOOKS IN SEA QUEST SERIES 7:

THE LOST STARSHIP

VELOTH
THE VAMPIRE SQUID

978 1 40834 064 6

GLENDOR
THE STEALTHY SHADOW

978 1 40834 066 0

MIRROC
THE GOBLIN SHARK

978 1 40834 068 4

BLISTRA
THE SEA DRAGON

978 1 40834 070 7

OUT NOW!

Look out for all the books in
Sea Quest Series 8:

THE LORD OF ILLUSION

GORT THE DEADLY SNATCHER

FANGOR THE CRUNCHING GIANT

SHELKA THE MIGHTY FORTRESS

LOOSEJAW THE NIGHTMARE FISH

OUT IN AUGUST 2016!

Don't miss the
BRAND NEW
Special Bumper Edition:

REPTA

THE SPIKED BRUTE

OUT IN JUNE 2016

WIN AN EXCLUSIVE
GOODY BAG

In every Sea Quest book the Sea Quest logo is hidden in one of the pictures. Find the logos in books 25-28, make a note of which pages they appear on and go online to enter the competition at

www.seaquestbooks.co.uk

Each month we will put all of the correct entries into a draw and select one winner to receive a special Sea Quest goody bag.

You can also send your entry on a postcard to:

Sea Quest Competition, Orchard Books,
Carmelite House, 50 Victoria Embankment,
London, EC4Y 0DZ

Don't forget to include your name and address!

GOOD LUCK

Closing Date: May 31st 2016

IF YOU LIKE SEA QUEST, YOU'LL LOVE BEAST QUEST!

Series 1: COLLECT THEM ALL!

An evil wizard has enchanted the magical beasts of Avantia. Only a true hero can free the beasts and save the land. Is Tom the hero Avantia has been waiting for?

FERNO
THE FIRE DRAGON

978 1 84616 483 5

SEPRON
THE SEA SERPENT

978 1 84616 482 8

ARCTA
THE MOUNTAIN GIANT

978 1 84616 484 2

TAGUS
THE HORSE-MAN

978 1 84616 486 6

NANOOK
THE SNOW MONSTER

978 1 84616 485 9

EPOS
THE FLAME BIRD

978 1 84616 487 3

DON'T MISS THE BRAND NEW SERIES OF: